CW00738929

To request permissions contact the publisher at
Info@kushitePublishing.com
Or
Info@BestBlackChildrensBooks.com

Hardcover: ISBN 979-8-9863746-6-6
Paperback: ISBN 979-8-9863746-9-7
Library of Congress Control Number: 2022910963

Edited by: Ismani Sun
Cover Art by: Ismani Sun
Layout by: Ismani Sun

Printed in the USA
Distributed by Kushite Publishing & Education

Publisher's Cataloging-in-Publication data

Names: Sun, Kushakti, author. | Sun, Ismani, illustrator.
Title: Summer in Grandpa's garden / written by Kushakti Sun; illustrated by Ismani Sun.
Description: Converse, TX: Kushite Publishing Company, 2022. | Summary: Grandpa Ogun teaches his grandson, Olumide, how to grow food in the garden.
Identifiers: LCCN: 2022910963 | ISBN: 979-8-9863746-6-6 (hardcover) | 979-8-9863746-9-7 (paperback)
Subjects: LCSH Gardening--Juvenile fiction. | Grandfathers--Juvenile fiction. | Grandparents and grandchildren--Juvenile fiction. | Family--Juvenile fiction. | African American children--Juvenile fiction. | African American families--Juvenile fiction. | BISAC JUVENILE FICTION / Science & Nature / Weather | JUVENILE FICTION / People & Places / United States / African American & Black | JUVENILE FICTION / Family / Multigenerational
Classification: LCC PZ7.1.S8578 Su 2022 | DDC [E]--dc23

Visit us at www.Kushitepublishing.com & www.BestBlackChildrensBooks.com

Summer in Grandpa's Garden

Written by KUSHAKTI SUN

Illustrated by ISMANI SUN

Today I'm going to help
Grandpa Ogun in the garden.

I'll get to plant seeds
for growing fruits
and vegetables.

Winter, spring, summer and fall make up the four seasons

Winter

Spring

But Spring and summer are the best time of the year to plant, a garden.

Summer

Fall

Grandpa says I will grow plants that can make the type of foods that I like to eat. Foods like strawberries and blueberries.

He allowed me to order the seeds
I wanted and soon after, a drone
delivered them right
above our garden.

Today I will teach you
the old ways young Olu,
“said Grandpa”.

First you till the soil.

Then you clear the weeds.

Next add plant food so they will grow strong and Healthy.

Soil has many layers, each play a unique role in a garden.

Top Soil

Sub Soil

Parent Material

Bedrock

The soil has a busy living ecosystem that help the plants thrive.

Next we make a hole
in the soil and drop
the seeds right in.

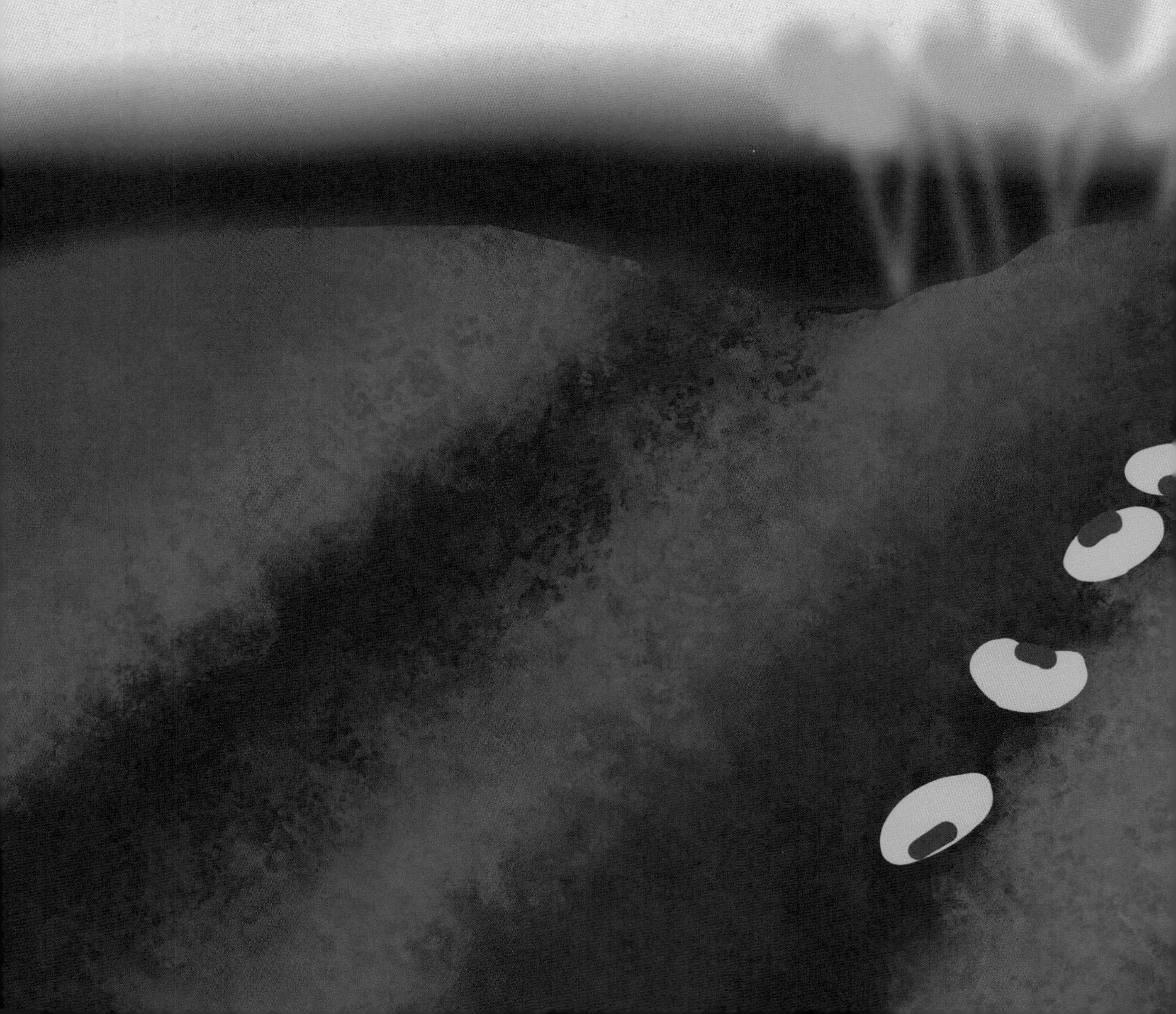

Everyday we water the seed and make sure the ground is wet.

Soon a sprout will come up.

Sprout-

-Leaf

Stem-

-Roots

The sprout soon turns into a plant with leaves.

Weeks go by and little flowers grow between the leaves.

PHOTOSYNTHESIS

Water

Light Energy

Oxygen

Carbon Dioxide

Sugars

Flowers are very important to a plant's life cycle.

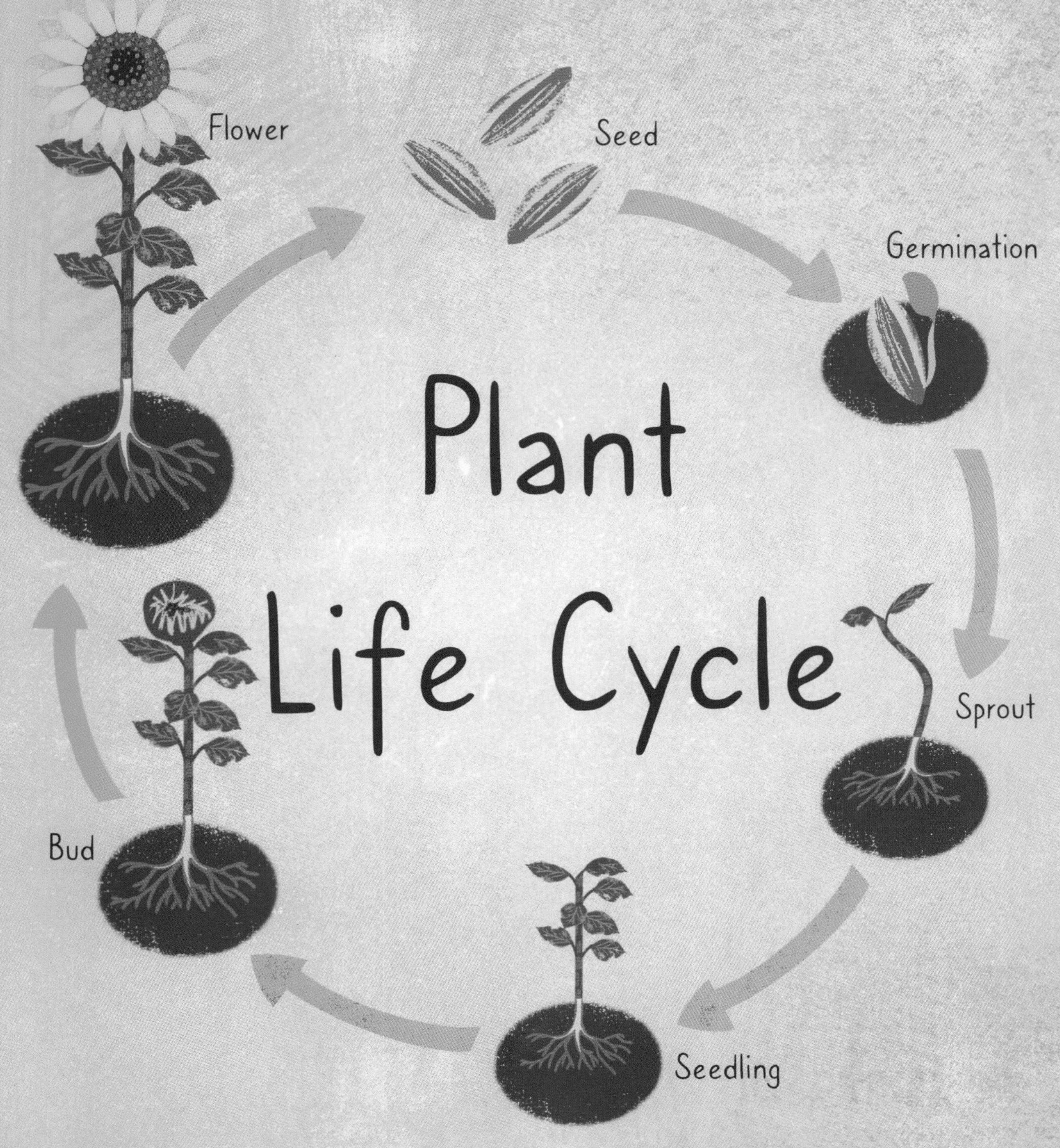

leaves help a plant produce energy.

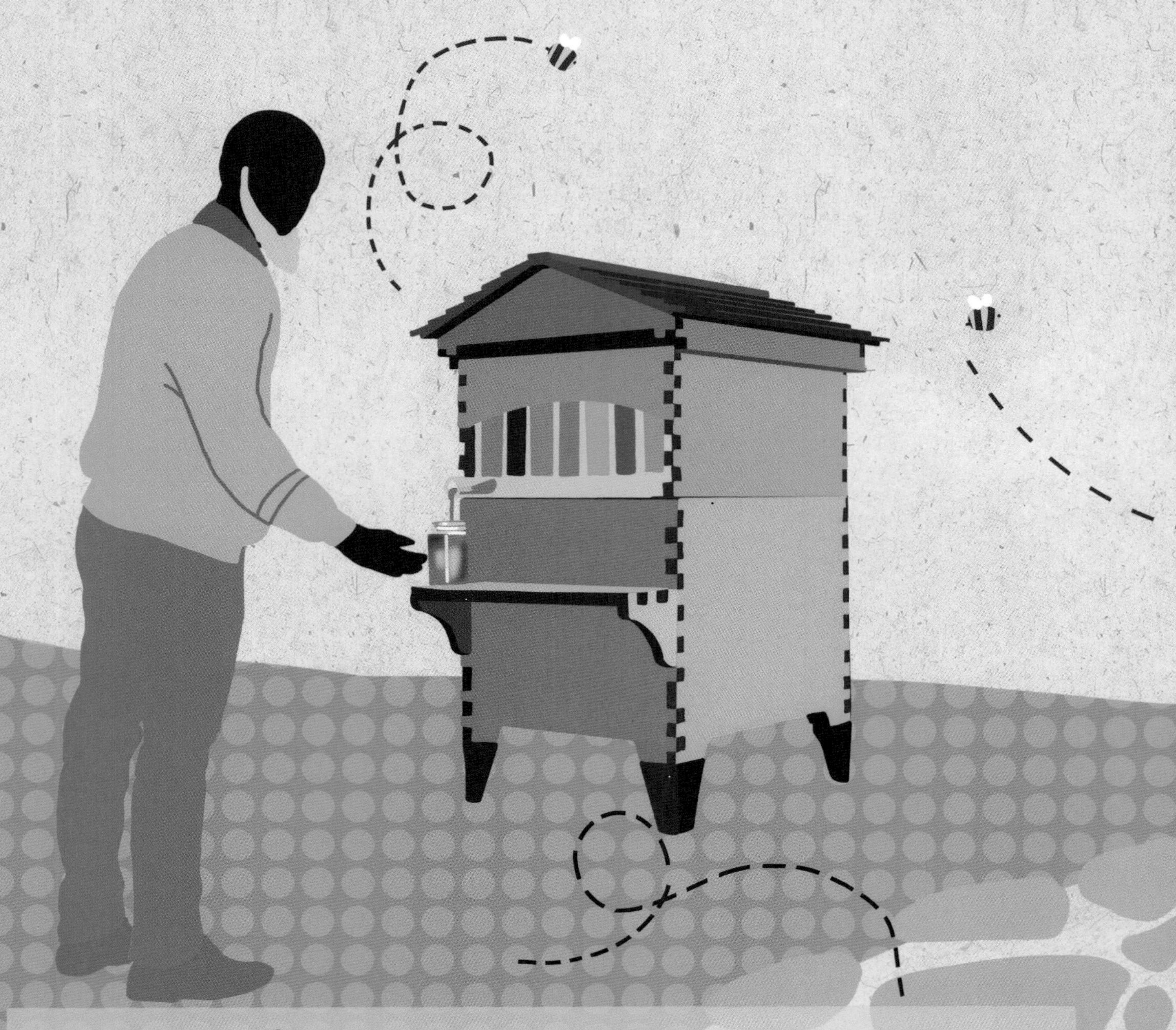

Grandpa's honey bees come
to pollinate the flowers.
One of the flowers starts
to turn into a watermelon.

Each week
it gets bigger
and **bigger**.

Little Garden helpers
pollinate the garden.

So more fruits
and veggies
can grow!

"Olu, your strawberries are ready to eat now,"
Said Grandpa.

I take a bowl
and pick the
biggest ones.
They are red,
juicy and sweet.

When the watermelon is ripe and ready, grandpa pulls it up and cuts a big piece for me to eat.

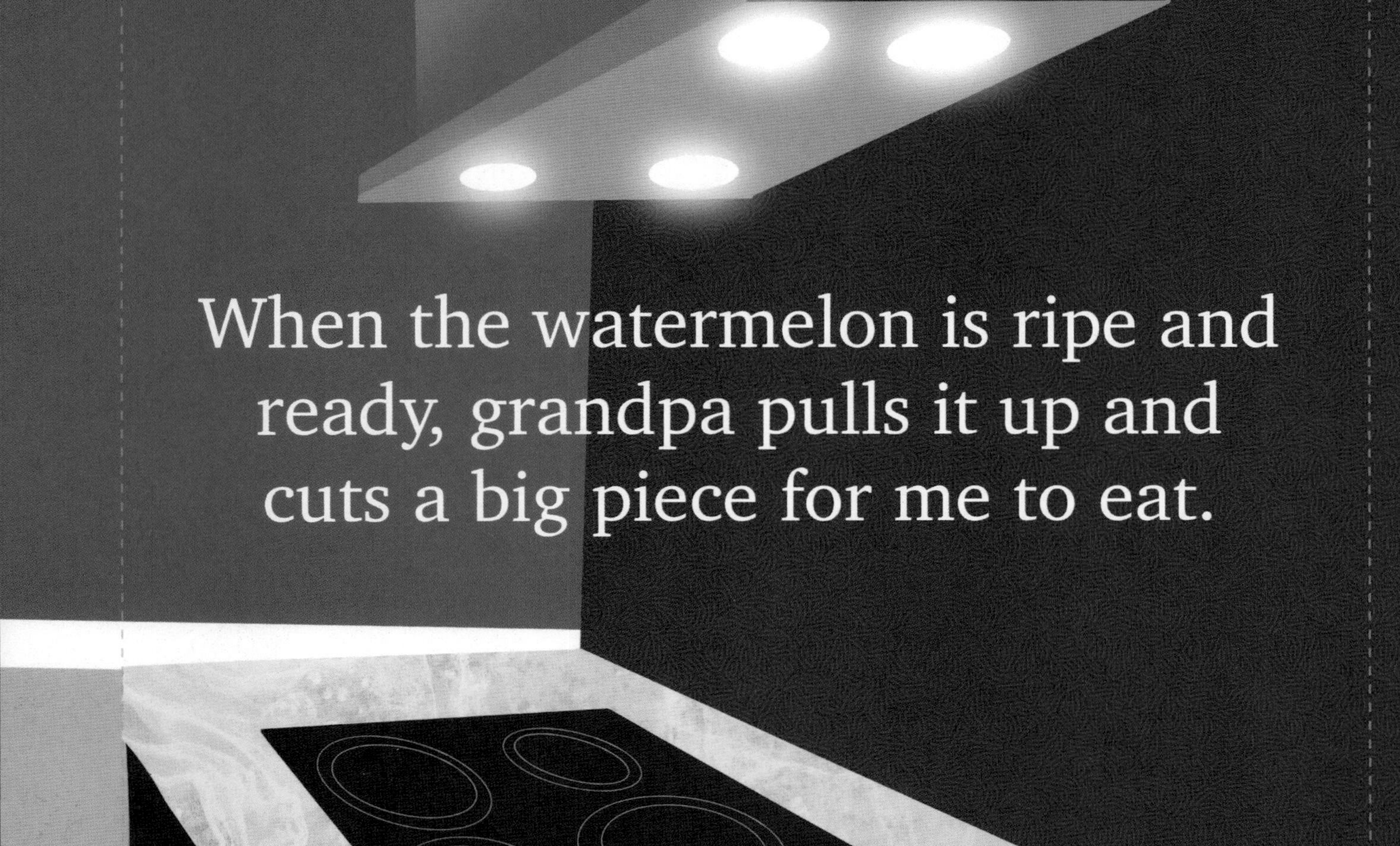

Summertime
is almost over

I'll be going home soon
with food that I grew
with grandpa!

Grandpa Ogun asks me what I've learned this summer, and then says he hopes he has taught me some of the old values in this new world.

The End.

OGUN CORP.

Scan to Donate

Printed in Great Britain
by Amazon